Sugar
and
Snails

By Sarah Tsiang   Art by Sonja Wimmer

annick press
toronto + berkeley

Designed by Sonja Wimmer and Sheryl Shapiro

Annick Press Ltd.

We acknowledge the support of the Canada Council for the Arts and the Ontario Arts Council, and the participation of the Government of Canada/la participation du gouvernement du Canada for our publishing activities.

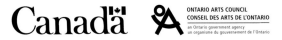

Library and Archives Canada Cataloging in Publication

Tsiang, Sarah, 1978-, author
          Sugar and snails / Sarah Tsiang ; illustrated by Sonja Wimmer.

Issued in print and electronic formats.
ISBN 978-1-77321-005-6 (hardcover).—ISBN 978-1-77321-004-9 (softcover).—
ISBN 978-1-77321-007-0 (PDF).—ISBN 978-1-77321-006-3 (HTML)

          I. Wimmer, Sonja, illustrator II. Title.

PS8639.S583S89 2018   jC811'.6   C2017-905594-1
                                                           C2017-905595-X

Published in the U.S.A. by Annick Press (U.S.) Ltd.
Distributed in Canada by University of Toronto Press.
Distributed in the U.S.A. by Publishers Group West.

Printed in China

www.annickpress.com
www.sarahtsiang.wordpress.com
www.sonjawimmer.com

Also available in e-book format.
Please visit www.annickpress.com/ebooks.html for more details.

For Natasha and Victoria, both of whom contain multitudes.
—S.T.

To Luna, who is made of the most wonderful things I can imagine.
—S.W.

What are little boys made of?
Frogs and Snails and Puppy Dogs' Tails.
What are little girls made of?
Sugar and Spice and Everything Nice.

Pass me the sugar,
would you?

Let's see. A little sugar, a pinch of spice, just like that old rhyme about sweet girls like you.

What about sweet boys like me?

Hmm. It's about boys and girls.
I think it goes like this:

What are little boys made of?
Pirates and dogs and noisy
bullfrogs.

What are little girls made of?
Dresses and sweets and
everything neat.

You don't, do you?
Okay, so boys are
made of cookies
and spice . . .

and jump-roping mice?

And girls are made of snails and rocks . . .

and butterfly socks!

Maybe it was
boys are made of lightning
and newts . . .

and rubber rain boots.

and dinosaur tails!

Maybe it was
boys are made of
balloons and mutts?

And fresh chicken butts!

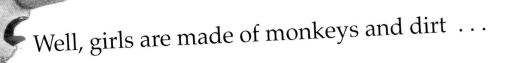

Well, girls are made of monkeys and dirt . . .

and lemon dessert.

Or it could be boys are made of flowers and swings . . .

and bumblebee wings!

And girls are made of
tires and slides and crazy-fast rides.

And some boys
are made of
marbles and fish
and all things
that squish.

And girls can
be made of
snake skins and
pies and bright
fireflies.

Dangnamit, I give up.
What in the heck are
you made of?

What are little boys made of?
Frogs and Snails and Pu
What are little girls made of?
Sugar and